"AN ANCIENT EGYPTIAN PROPHECY AND A
CHALLENGING QUEST TO FREE THE GODS – IF YOU
LIKE AN EPIC ADVENTURE STORY COMBINED WITH
GREAT ILLUSTRATIONS, YOU'LL LOVE THIS."

DR JULIE ANDERSON,
DEPARTMENT OF ANCIENT EGYPT AND SUDAN
THE BRITISH MUSEUM

With thanks to Adrian Bott

First published in the UK in 2013 by Usborne Publishing Ltd.,
Usborne House, 83-85 Saffron Hill, London EC1N 8RT, England.
www.usborne.com

Text copyright © Hothouse Fiction, 2013

Illustrations copyright © Usborne Publishing Ltd., 2013

Cover illustration by Jerry Paris. Inside illustrations by David Shephard.
Map by Ian McNee.

With thanks to Anne Millard for historical consultancy.

The name Usborne and the devices ♀ ♛ are Trade Marks of
Usborne Publishing Ltd.

A CIP catalogue record for this book is available from the British Library.

ISBN 9781409562054   JFM MJJASOND/13 02928/1
Printed in Dongguan, Guangdong, China.

INTO THE UNDERWORLD

USBORNE

QUEST of the GODS

SCREAM OF THE
BABOON KING

DAN HUNTER

USBORNE

THE SACRED COFFIN TEXT OF PHARAOH AKORI

I SHALL SAIL RIGHTLY IN MY VESSEL
I AM LORD OF ETERNITY
IN THE CROSSING OF THE SKY.

LET MY HEART SPEAK TRUTH;
LET ME NOT SUFFER
THE TORMENTS OF THE WICKED!

FOR THE GREAT DEVOURER AWAITS,
AND THE FORTY-TWO DEMONS
HOWL AROUND THE HALL OF JUDGEMENT.

LET ME HOLD MY HEAD UPRIGHT IN HONOUR,
AND BE SPARED THE CLAWS AND TEETH
OF THE SHRIEKING ONES.

THE EATERS OF BONES,
LET THEM NOT TOUCH ME.
THE DRINKERS OF BLOOD,
LET THEM NOT COME NEAR ME.
THE WINGED ONES WITH JAWS OF IRON,
MAY THEY PASS ME BY.

AND MAY I REMAIN SAFE
IN THE PRESENCE OF OSIRIS FOREVER.

PROLOGUE

The demon-boy, Oba, stood on top of the
highest tower of his palace, gazing out over
the Underworld. An endless plain of bones
and debris lay before him, lit by huge fires.
Animal-headed beings herded dead souls into
pens, taunting them cruelly before throwing
them into pits.

Oba liked to watch the suffering. The
wonderful thing about tormenting the dead
was that it could never end. And besides,
it would teach them to respect him as their
new lord and master. He had been watching
the fire and agony for hours, and would
never grow tired of it.

Back when he had been ruler of Egypt,
his sleep had either been deep and peaceful,

or filled with glorious dreams of taking more and more power. He remembered how he would awake, still clutching his fingers around the arms of some golden throne that only existed in his fantasies, and go raging through his palace in a wild fury because he was only Pharaoh of Egypt and not of the whole world.

Occasionally the face of his father would torment him, giving him nightmares – the father he had murdered with cobra venom, so that he could steal the Egyptian throne for himself. Then Oba would wake screaming, not because he regretted murdering his father, but because he feared the old man had come back to reclaim what was rightfully his.

Those nightmares never happened now, because Oba was no longer mortal and no longer needed to sleep. Thanks to Set's magic, the blood that ran in his veins was now laced with fire. It filled him with endless energy, making his eyes shine in the half-light like a predator's, giving him the power to work dark magic of his own.

Sleep was for the weak, he thought to himself. Only pathetic human fools like his arch-enemy Akori needed sleep.

"You!" he said to a passing shabti, a grotesque Underworld servant made from blue wax. "What time is it in the living world?"

"Mighty One, it is midnight," the shabti replied, his waxen face melting slightly in the heat from the fire.

Oba smiled. Almost all of Egypt would be asleep now – those that could sleep, at any rate. He and his master Set had been amassing their army of the undead now for many days and already they had begun to rise from their tombs.

Let Egypt try to sleep through the sound of graves bursting open from within! Let the people try to sleep while ragged fingernails went scratch, scratch, scratch *on the doors of their houses.*

"Oh, Egypt," Oba gloated, "your poor farm boy Akori cannot help you now. Soon you will beg for the days when I was your Pharaoh. And those prayers will be answered. Soon I will return to rule you again...but I will make you suffer for your betrayal!"

"Will that be all, Master?" the shabti grovelled.

"No," Oba said. "Prepare the flame. I wish to view the world of the living."

"At once!" the shabti said. It marched off into the inner chambers of the palace. Oba followed behind, past galleries that echoed with screams and over bridges that spanned nightmarishly deep pits.

The flame lay at the heart of Oba's sanctuary, a room that bore the darkest of images on the walls. It burned in a broad copper dish encrusted with black stones. Ordinarily, it shone with a feeble bluish light, but the right spells could kindle it into a raging inferno of magical power.

The shabti knew what to do. It threw fistfuls of purple dust into the flame, making it roar up, no longer feeble but a towering pillar of fire. The shabti staggered back from the fire, obviously terrified.

"Leave me," Oba told it, his voice thick with contempt. Oba's hands moved in strange, sinuous gestures. He mouthed the words of power that Set had taught him.

"Powers of evil!" Oba called, raising his hands. "Powers of eternal night, you who serve my ally Set, God of Darkness! Show me Akori!"

The image of Akori asleep in a sumptuous bed appeared in a flame-framed window. The room where he slept was aglow with golden fittings and tables nearby were heaped with fruit and flowers. A window stood unshuttered, letting in a gentle night breeze that stirred the silken hangings.

Oba scowled, feeling the force of his hatred rise. When he had been Pharaoh, that room had been a stifling, dark chamber where all the servants were afraid to go. He barely recognized it now.

Oba's hate burned even more strongly when he saw Akori had set up little shrines to the Gods of Egypt who were loyal to Horus, along the wall of his bedchamber. Those Gods had been Oba's downfall. They would all suffer, every one.

For Oba had Gods of his own to call upon now. At the far end of the hall something huge stood in the shadows. The dancing light revealed little of its shape, but whatever it was, it was hunched over and covered with coarse fur. Two red pinpricks of fire gleamed from its eyes.

"Do you see?" Oba demanded of it, pointing to Akori. "How he sleeps so soundly, as if nothing was wrong?"

The creature's answer was a low growl, like the rattle of a chain being dragged from a deep well.

"He is your prey!" Oba said. "He is the one I want you to kill!"

The creature reared up in the darkness and gave a roar of excitement that shook the whole hall like an earthquake. The fire flared up – and just for a second Oba saw the face of the thing he was about to unleash on Akori. For that one second, he was afraid of it. Then he remembered who was in control.

Suddenly the flames roared upwards with fresh fury, interrupting Oba's gloating. The image of Akori vanished. In its place was a titanic figure, with the head of a beast like a monstrous boar. It roared in anger.

"Set!" Oba stammered, stepping back. "My Dark Lord."

"Spare me your pleasantries," Set raged. "Twice now you have let Akori escape death! How?"

"My Lord," Oba whined, "Baal was stupid, and Sokar's nerve failed us!"

"You blame your allies?" Set boomed. "Perhaps the blame lies...with you. I preserved your life when Akori's blade split your chest open. Maybe I should undo my work?"

"No!" Oba protested. "We will not fail again, I swear it!"

"Make sure you do not," Set warned him

fiercely. "Remember, I can crush you like a gnat."

"Believe me, My Lord," Oba panted, "Akori will not survive. When my new friend is finished with him, he will be torn to shreds. There will be nothing left."

"Nothing?" Set rumbled.

"Not even a fingernail!"

The creature in the shadows gave a murderous screech...

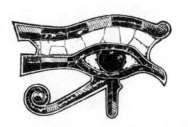

CHAPTER ONE

Akori groaned in his sleep. He rolled over in sheets soaked with sweat. Usually the dreams he had were of green fields, rivers running and bringing fertility to the land. But tonight's dream was very different. He stood in a field of wheat, but the sun in the sky was a blood-red orb and there was a nasty smell in the air. He knew, with the deep horrible certainty that nightmares bring, that *something* was in his chamber with him, a lurking presence behind him waiting to pounce.

He knew he had a job to do. Was he supposed to reap the wheat? Uncle Shenti would be angry with him if he didn't do his work. He looked down at the sickle he held. It was ancient and looked as if it had been neglected for years.

"I can't do any good with this!" he said to himself in his dream. His words seemed to echo back at him, mocking him.

Now the sickle changed, becoming his golden *khopesh*, the gift of Horus – but in his dream it was nothing but a wooden toy. The gold was only paint.

"No!" he moaned in his sleep. "Not... real..."

His dream enfolded him like a shroud. There was no escaping it. He stood in the wheatfield, armed with the useless wooden sword, and now the earth began to cave in around him. Holes were appearing all over the place. Grey, skinny arms emerged writhing from the holes, giving Akori the same sickening feeling of watching a maggot emerging from a rotten fig.

The dead were clawing their way up to the surface from the Underworld! All at once, he remembered what had happened, what the threat to Egypt was. Oba and Set had launched their attack on the living world and he had failed in his duty to protect his people. The undead army was rising!

He threw the useless toy sword away. Hadn't Horus given him some armour to wear? He looked down and saw nothing but a farmer's smock, threadbare and useless.

The dead were pulling themselves up from the crumbling earth, reaching for Akori with clutching hands. A chorus of moans rang out all around him, the cry of the dead hungry for revenge on the living. He turned to run, but the earth seemed to suck at his feet, dragging him down.

The thing that was waiting and watching was much closer now, he knew. As he ran, Akori could sense it behind him, but he couldn't turn around. If he did, it would all be over.

The thing was gaining on him. He heard it give a screech of triumph, the unmistakable sound of a beast about to seize and tear at its prey. He screamed and fell as the weight of the thing came crashing down on his back. Clammy hands grabbed his arm. He knew the thing would tear it right out of its socket.

With a yell and a gasp, Akori was suddenly awake. For a second he had no idea where he was, then the familiar features of the room struck him, along with a horrible realization.

The thing was still clutching his arm. He could feel its tight grip.

The nightmare had followed him into the waking world. He grabbed the arm that was holding his, rolled out of bed with a yell and heaved the thing's body right over him, sending it sprawling across the floor.

"Aaagh!" Manu yelled as he flailed about. "Akori, it's me! What are you doing?"

Akori shook his head, desperately trying to clear it of the sleep that still clung. "Oh, by the Gods! I didn't mean to – oh Manu, I'm so sorry!"

Akori held a hand out. Manu took it and let Akori help him to his feet. "What *happened*?" he asked. "I thought you'd been bewitched."

"I was having a nightmare," Akori said. "It seemed so real. The dead were rising from the Underworld, and there was something else, something trying to kill me. Something I couldn't see..."

"Akori," Manu said, his eyes wide with concern. "There's a real-life nightmare going on right now."

Akori hurriedly pulled on his clothes. "What's happening?"

"We're under attack!" Manu replied.

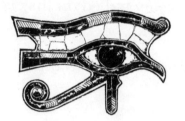

CHAPTER TWO

Akori stared at Manu. "Under attack?
From who?" He pulled his golden armoured
tunic over his head. Two of the Pharaoh
Stones, the jewels of Courage and Speed,
glowed in the breastplate. Had his dream
been a prophecy of what was to come? If so,
was the unseen, growling thing here too?

"I was up in the tower checking the
positions of the stars, to make sure we
picked the luckiest time to go on our next
quest," Manu said, "and I saw an army

marching towards the palace. I didn't get a proper look at them," he admitted. "I came straight to tell you."

Ebe the cat bounded in through the door and stood there with her fur bristling. A thin blue mist was following her down the corridor, rolling over the flagstones like a rug. Ebe gave a long mournful mew.

Akori grabbed his *khopesh* from the stand by his bed. "If we're under attack, then where are all the guards? Why didn't you go to the captain?"

Manu shook his head. "The guards are all asleep."

"Asleep?" Akori yelled, aghast. "Why didn't you wake them up?"

"I tried!" Manu wailed. "I couldn't even get them to open their eyes!"

"What about the High Priest?" asked Akori, panicked.

"Him too!" replied Manu.

Ebe dabbed her paw into the crawling mist, scurried back quickly and mewed again. Akori ran to the door. All the way up the torchlit passage, he saw guards sitting slumped in their seats.

"It must be a spell," Akori said. "Oba's behind this, I'm sure of it! He's sent this mist to put my guards to sleep."

"So his servants can attack us without anyone coming to help!" Manu agreed. "But that means..."

"We're going to have to fight them on our own," said Akori. "Come on, quickly!"

Together they raced to the front door of the palace. The mist around their feet was freezing cold. Akori had to wonder if they, too, would succumb to its effects.

"Why doesn't the mist send *us* to sleep?" he asked Manu as they ran.

"The nice possibility," Manu gasped, "is that the Good Gods are protecting us. The nasty possibility is that whoever's doing this wants us to suffer through every minute!"

Akori shoved open the great double doors that led outside. The moon was bright overhead, shining down into the open courtyard and clearly revealing an army of pale blue figures. They stood in a perfect square formation, as if someone had arranged them carefully.

The moonlight glistened on their waxy, expressionless faces. Then they all took one stiff step forwards and stamped down hard on the ground – *boom.*

"What are they?" he asked Manu.

"They're shabtis," Manu said, a tremor of fear in his voice. "Mindless servants sworn to obey. Wealthy people are buried with them. They're just wax figures in the living world, but when you're buried and your soul crosses over, they go with you and come to life. Then they're your servants for ever."

The shabti army took another relentless step forward.

Akori's heart sank. If these things only came to life *in* the Underworld, then they must have entered Egypt *from* the Underworld. That meant Oba was behind this – and if his servants were breaking through already, his evil plan must be taking shape.

"I'll send them back to the Underworld in bits!" he snarled.

As the army advanced again, taking another jerky step, Akori leaped forward and swung his *khopesh* at the nearest shabti. The blade bit deep into the thing's waxy body, slicing all the way through and out the other side. It was like hacking through soft fat.

But to Akori's horror he saw the sword cut was healing shut! He hadn't damaged the shabti at all. The wax it was made of was simply flowing back together.

He sliced again, hacking the thing's arm off.

The shabti calmly picked the arm back up with its remaining hand and held it to its shoulder, like a servant picking up a dropped broom. The arm instantly fused back to the body.

"I can't hurt it!" Akori told Manu desperately. "How do you kill something that's never even been alive?"

Before Manu could answer, one shabti, bigger than the others, raised its arm in the midst of the throng. It pointed to Akori. "TAKE HIM," it croaked.

"Back to the palace!" Akori shouted.

Ebe darted through the doors, and Akori

and Manu heaved them shut just as the shabtis charged forwards. Akori drew the bolt across the doors. The entire hall felt like it was shaking as two dozen waxen blue fists pounded on them.

"Akori, we need to think," Manu said. "How do you fight *wax*?"

Akori looked back down the hall, to where the sleeping guards were slumped under the torches. The dancing flames gave him an idea. "Manu, grab a torch. Let's see if they can shrug *fire* off!"

He and Manu stood side by side, torches in their hands. Ebe skulked behind them, looking like she was ready to pounce. Akori took a deep breath and slid the bolt back on the doors.

The shabtis marched in with a rhythmic stomp. There was something unnerving and horrible about the way their mask-like faces never changed expression, even when they reached up for Akori and Manu, trying to clutch them around the neck and choke the life out of them.

Akori shoved his torch deep into a shabti's body. Its waxy form collapsed as the hot brand slid into it, caving in and liquefying. The shabti waggled its hands jerkily like a man having a fit. Next moment, the whole thing burst into flames.

The other shabtis lurched back from it, as if they knew it was dangerous. Akori kicked the burning creature into the courtyard and it exploded into flaming chunks that scattered through the other shabtis like missiles. A few more caught fire as the flaming debris landed on them and they tottered drunkenly back through their comrades.

Meanwhile, Manu was jabbing at the shabtis near him, trying to drive them back.

They seemed less afraid of his torch than they were of Akori's. One of them got a grip on Manu's throat and lifted him off the floor.

Ebe sprang forwards with a yowl, distracting it, and Manu thrust his torch into the shabti's face. It instantly melted into a runny blue ruin, spattering molten wax on the palace floor.

The shabti released its grip and fell backwards like a toppling tree, leaving Manu gasping for breath. It spattered into bits.

"Drive them all back into the courtyard!" Akori yelled. "Set as many on fire as you can!"

"I'm doing my best!" Manu panted. "But it's hard to set something on fire when it's— *argh!*"

Another shabti was attacking Manu, arms flailing in his face. It knocked the torch from his grasp. Ebe shook herself and transformed into her full size, becoming a giant wildcat. She launched herself at the creature and pushed it back into the others, sending them scattering like skittles in a child's game. The shabtis were packed so close together and in such orderly formation that only a few were left standing.

Akori ran around the heap of fallen shabtis, setting fire to one after another until the whole army had become a single flaming mass. Thick black smoke poured up from them.

Yells were going up from the palace corridors. "The guards!" Manu exclaimed. "They're awake!"

"The spell must have been broken," Akori said triumphantly. "Good job we set these things on fire out here in the courtyard. The way they're burning, the whole palace might have gone up!"

Some of the shabtis were still moving amid the roaring flames, but they were losing their humanoid shape even as Akori watched. Arms melted down to stubs, heads collapsed like rotten fruit and bodies fell apart and turned to pools of flickering molten wax.

The guards came running up, shielding their eyes from the blaze. "My Pharaoh," the guard captain blurted out, "I'm sorry, I don't know what happened! I take full responsibility!"

"It's all right, Captain," Akori assured him. "There wasn't anything you could have done. Dark magic was at work here tonight." He smiled. "But now you're here you can help us put the fire out."

Suddenly one of the guards shouted. "Look at the flames!" he yelled. "Something's appearing in them – something huge!"

CHAPTER THREE

Akori stared. The guard was right. The
shabtis were nothing but a pool of blue wax
now, but the fire was still burning brighter
then ever and it was forming into a massive,
overbearing figure. The light concentrated
itself into the shape of a man, tall and
powerful, with a hawk's head. Akori knew
that figure well.

"Horus!" Akori shouted in delight.

"Well fought, my champion," said the
God. Beside him, the guards thumped their

chests in welcome and sank to one knee.

"There is no time to lose!" Horus warned. "Akori, you must leave for the Underworld immediately. Oba and Set have gained power since you fought them last."

"I knew it as soon as I saw the shabtis," Akori said. "Those things belong in the Underworld, don't they?"

"They do," Horus said. "Oba is steadily destroying the barriers that divide the Underworld from the world of the living. More and more creatures from the Underworld are able to escape their prison and attack the living world. First came the bewitched dead, and now those who are meant to serve the dead." Horus's voice boomed with a terrible sudden anger. "Oba and Set are profaning the sacred order of things, the order my father Osiris has kept for thousands of years. This obscenity must end, Akori."

"I shall end it," Akori promised. This was his sworn quest. As the champion of Horus, he had agreed to go into the Underworld and retrieve the five Pharaoh Stones, powerful magical jewels that Osiris, the rightful ruler f the Underworld, had been guarding. Each one was connected to one of the Pharaoh's virtues: courage, strength, speed, honour and intelligence. They were meant to be used by a Pharaoh who was worthy to bear them. But when Set had overthrown Osiris, Oba had stolen the Pharaoh Stones. Unable to use them himself, he had given them to his monstrous servants so that they could feed on their power.

Akori had won the Stones of Courage and Speed on his recent quests to the Underworld and he could feel their power through his armour, one burning hot like a coal, the other thrumming and vibrating with energy.

There were still three more Stones to find before Akori would be strong enough to confront Set and Oba. He yearned to confront them *now*, though. Akori dreamed of a surprise attack on Oba, when the boy least expected it. If they could only find a secret way into the heart of the Underworld, and ambush Oba. Set might have saved Oba's life after the last time they had met, but Akori wasn't about to let Oba get away again.

"You must enter the Underworld at once," Horus told him.

"But we can't!" Akori was suddenly confused. "My Lord, it's the middle of the night! Aken's boat only crosses over at sunset. That's not for hours yet."

"Aken's boat is the safest way into the Underworld," Horus explained, "but it is not the only way. There are gates, hidden passages, caverns that run deep below Egypt. Oba and Set know about most of them and have placed guards there. But there is one entrance known only to me and my father."

"Where is it?" Akori asked, amazed to think there had been other ways to the Underworld all along.

"In ancient times, there was a Pharaoh so evil and corrupt that his name was obliterated from history," Horus said. "He built a secret doorway to the Underworld, hoping to lead his enslaved followers to the Judgement Hall of Osiris and overthrow him."

"Just like Oba!" Akori exclaimed.

"Indeed. Unlike Oba, the Dark Pharaoh did not have Set as an ally, and his attack failed. But the doorway he built to reach my father's hall is still there, buried deep within the palace."

"I thought the Dark Pharaoh was just a legend," Manu said hollowly. "When I was younger, the other trainee priests told me about a sealed-up room in the palace, where there were busts of a man with his face chiselled off, and his name scratched out on the tablets. I thought they were making it up to scare me!"

"It is no legend," Horus said firmly. "The route through the Ruined Palace of the Dark Pharaoh is perilous, but we have no choice. You must reach the Underworld as quickly as you can." He passed Akori a thick scroll. "Thoth, God of Wisdom, has prepared this for you. The instructions will help you travel swiftly to your destination, and the spells will give you what protection the Gods can provide. Your old High Priest of Horus has recovered from the magic spell. He shall protect Egypt in your absence."

"Thank you," Akori said gratefully, taking the scroll.

"Good luck, my champion," said Horus. "Now hurry!" He vanished from sight, and the flames died away. All of the shabtis had disappeared.

"Akori," Manu said casually, "can I have a look at that scroll, please?"

Akori passed it to his friend. Manu unrolled it, wide-eyed. "Incantations from the Book of Thoth itself," he squeaked. "Written by the very hand of the Ibis-Headed One. Akori, this is a priceless treasure. We have to keep it safe."

"It's meant to help us in our quest, not sit in a library," Akori laughed. "Horus said there were spells. Can you read them?"

"Oh, yes," Manu breathed. "The first one is a travelling spell, to bring us to the Ruined Palace of the Dark Pharaoh."

"Well, what are you waiting for? Read it."
Akori held out his torch to cast light on the parchment.

Manu began to read the words. As he got to the very last syllable, Akori felt a bizarre floating sensation in his stomach as the palace dissolved around them. There was a brief feeling of tumbling through space, the moon and stars spinning madly, before they landed suddenly with a thump. Akori and Manu went sprawling. Only Ebe landed with anything like dignity, squarely on her four paws.

Akori's first thought was: *Thank the Gods I kept hold of my torch!*

Only the torch's flame gave any light in the dark chamber they stood in. It was the shattered ruin of a temple. Akori saw the stony debris that littered the floor was covered with hieroglyphics, meaning they

had once covered the walls. Eerie, faceless statues of unknown Gods surrounded them. Akori wondered what they had looked like, then decided he'd just as soon not know.

"Bring that light over here, Akori!" Manu said. "I think this is the secret door!"

Akori held the torch so Manu could trace the outlines of a huge stone slab. "This is it, all right," Manu said. "According to the scroll, these words should open it. I just hope it still works after all this time."

"Just so long as the spell doesn't summon anything by accident," Akori said with a shudder. "This is a cursed place. It feels like nobody's set foot here in a thousand years!"

Ebe mewed in agreement. She slunk in close and rubbed herself around Akori's leg.

Manu chanted the spell and the slab began to move. Slowly it edged out of the wall, like a stone colossus advancing on them.

The slab ground forwards until it came all the way out. Akori couldn't believe how much easier this entrance into the Underworld was, as he watched the block of stone slide further, leaving a small gap. Akori was just imagining how the third Stone would look in his armour when there was an ugly grinding sound. Then, without warning, the slab of stone stopped dead.

"The spell failed!" Manu wailed. "Now there's no way into the Underworld!"

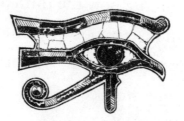

CHAPTER FOUR

Akori dashed over to the slab, trying to
remain calm. He pulled and tugged against
it, but it barely budged. Manu read the spell
again, but nothing happened.

"I think the spell only works once,"
Manu said sadly. "Now we're stuck here."

"We're not giving up that easily," Akori
said. "If magic won't shift it the rest of the
way, then muscle will have to. Help me
move the slab." Propping his torch against
the wall, he gripped the slab's edge with

both hands, then heaved.

Nothing happened at all. The muscles in his upper arms burned, but the slab didn't even budge.

"Come on, Manu! Help!"

Reluctantly, Manu joined him, hooking his fingers around the edge of the slab. Manu was as skinny as a skewer, but Akori knew any help he could give was better than none.

Manu heaved with all his might. It was a heroic effort, but it just wasn't enough.

"We need a lever of some sort," Manu panted.

Maybe the khopesh would work... Akori shoved his golden sword into the crack and worked it back and forth until it was wedged there. Now he just had to haul on it as hard as he could.

"Your sword?" Manu said doubtfully. "Won't it bend? Or break?"

"I don't think it can," Akori said, hoping in his heart that he was right.

He braced himself and pulled on the sword, wrenching it with every ounce of his strength. The slab still didn't budge.

Frustration built inside Akori, giving him fresh strength. He roared with the pain of the effort and pulled even harder.

There was the tiniest of grating sounds. "It's moving!" Manu yelled. "Harder, Akori!"

Akori set his feet against the wall, so he could push with his legs at the same time as hauling with his arms, as if he were hauling on a colossal oar. *I used to lift heavy loads on Uncle Shenti's farm all the time,* he thought. *I was a farm boy before I was a Pharaoh. These muscles of mine didn't come from sitting on a throne all day!*

Mentally he counted one, two, three...then he let out a mighty roar and *heaved,* using the full force of his arms and legs at once.

From nothing more than Akori's sheer brute force and willpower, the slab began to move. The sound was like a giant's teeth grinding together.

He clenched his jaw and kept pulling until there was enough of a gap for them to squeeze through, then he let go and fell to the ground, exhausted and gasping for breath.

"That was amazing," Manu said, helping him up. "I didn't think you were going to manage it."

"Thanks...Manu," Akori wheezed, exhausted from the effort. He gathered up his *khopesh* in one hand and the torch in the other. "Let's see what's on the other side."

After a painful squeeze for both Akori and Manu – Ebe slipped through easily – the trio found themselves in a dark tunnel that sloped steeply downwards. Akori held up his torch, revealing alcoves on either side of the tunnel that held dusty burial goods.

"These look like offerings for a tomb," Manu said. "I don't recognize any of the statuettes, though. Urgh. They're hideous."

In the flickering torchlight, the deformed statues seemed to watch them as they passed, willing them to slip and be sucked into the suffocating darkness below.

"Maybe the Dark Pharaoh had his own Gods..." Akori muttered.

"Look, there's an empty mummy case," Manu said. "I wonder who was meant to be buried in it?"

"Never mind that – we've no time to explore! What does the scroll say we're to do next?"

"We have to 'descend the path that slopes many long leagues below'," Manu read.

Akori looked at the tunnel ahead of them. It was sloping, all right – *sheer* would be another word for it. It was smooth, too. The stone, black as onyx, looked almost slippery. They'd have to walk carefully, taking care not to fall head over heels into the darkness. And if there were many leagues of tunnel to get through, it would take hours.

He fingered the Stone of Speed and looked around, wondering if there was a better way to do this. Then a smile spread over his face. "Manu, I've got an idea."

"It always worries me when you say that," Manu said. "What is it this time?"

Not long after, they sat together in the open mummy case, fetched down from the alcove where it had lain for the Gods only knew how long. Akori was in front, holding Ebe in his arms, while Manu sat at the back shaking his head. Akori had dug his *khopesh* into a crack in the ground to act as a brake.

"This is completely insane," Manu whispered.

"We'll get there quicker, won't we?"

"Well, yes, but—"

"Then let's do this!" Akori pulled the *khopesh* free, slipped it back into its hilt, and then tugged at the wall to get the mummy case moving.

It began to slide, slowly but surely, down the steep slope. Manu gave a deep groan and covered his eyes.

The mummy case began to pick up speed, until it was shooting down the tunnel slope like a runaway chariot. Manu yelled, the torch flames flew in the wind, Ebe flattened her ears and yowled and Akori roared out loud with excitement. The rock walls flickered past too quickly to see.

"It's working!" Akori shouted. "We'll be at the bottom in no time!"

"YES, BUT HOW ARE WE GOING TO STOP?" Manu bawled at him.

Akori hadn't thought of that. He clutched the ancient wood of the mummy case with one hand and held on tight to Ebe with the other. Her claws dug into his arm in her panic. They were flying down the tunnel now, faster and faster, completely out of control. A hot wind was blowing in his face from whatever lay ahead. Were his eyes playing tricks on him, or was that a light in the distance?

"Look!" Manu shrieked.

Akori saw what he meant. There was an opening up ahead – and they were going to fly through it faster than an arrow! What were they going to do?

Something Horus had once told him when

the God had first given him the *khopesh* flashed into his mind. "The blade is enchanted and will cut through iron and stone..."

Akori pushed Ebe into Manu's arms, leaned past him and drove the *khopesh* into the stone tunnel floor as hard as he could. The magical blade dug into the stone like a plough, carving a deep furrow and sending a spray of brilliant sparks up in their wake.

The sword was almost torn out of Akori's hands, but he held on with every remaining scrap of strength he had. Gradually, the speeding mummy case slowed down, with the golden sword acting like an anchor. The opening loomed up ahead. There was nothing beyond it – just a deep drop. Akori closed his eyes and held his breath.

When the mummy case finally ground to a halt, it was dangling over the very edge of the sheer drop. A hair's breadth more and they would have fallen into the chasm. Manu climbed out, giddily, and sat down on the firm ground. He stroked Ebe for a moment, calming both their nerves.

"Akori?" he said.

"Yes?"

"Let's never, *ever* do that again."

"Agreed," Akori said. He glanced back, looking at the huge gash his sword had carved through solid stone, and had to grin a little.

Once everyone had recovered, they cautiously climbed down from the tunnel mouth and out into the open space of a bleak, craggy valley.

"We're in the Underworld now, aren't we?" he asked.

Manu consulted the scroll. "Yes. Very much so. I don't think there's *ever* been a faster trip into the Underworld than that. Except dying, of course."

"It's much hotter here than the other places we've been," Akori said. "What does that mean?"

"It means we're nearing the heart of the Underworld," Manu said.

Ebe gave an urgent mew, attracting their attention. She was staring across the valley to where a group of small figures were huddled together.

Akori squinted, trying to see. They had lost the torch in the tunnel, and there was practically no light down here except for a dim red glow from some of the Underworld rocks, running through them like blood-coloured veins. "What are those things?"

"I can't tell in this light," Manu said. "But look, there's some more of them!"

The creatures were standing no more than ten metres away, with their backs to the group. A strange whispering and chattering came from the huddle.

Akori crept closer and beckoned to the others to follow. They all hunkered down behind a rock, peeping over the top at the labouring creatures.

"They look like children," Manu whispered to Akori.

He'd had the same thought. But then the "children" turned round. Horror struck Akori like a physical blow as he saw their inhuman faces. They weren't children at all. They were hunched-over baboons, with bared and bloody fangs!

As one, the baboons screeched aloud, dropped to all fours, and charged across the rocks. Akori held his breath. They were coming straight at him!

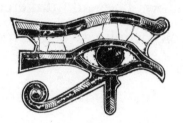

CHAPTER FIVE

Manu snatched up a rock and threw it at
an oncoming baboon, knocking it sprawling.
As the creature scrambled back to its feet,
he turned to Akori. "What do we do? There
are hundreds of them!"

Akori pointed to a hill of rubble that
looked like a burial cairn. "Up there! We
can make a stand on the high ground!"

Together, with the baboons close on their
heels, they charged across the broken,
uneven terrain. Ebe and Manu went

scrambling up the slope to the top of the hill, while Akori backed up behind them, brandishing his *khopesh* threateningly. The baboons advanced, sniffed the air, made chittering noises and advanced again.

All across the valley, baboons were taking notice of the others' calls. Heads popped up as the baboons scrambled over to attack. The ones near Akori made a high screeching noise, which was echoed by the oncoming ones.

"They're talking to each other!" Manu said, half in awe and half in fear. "What kind of baboon does that?"

"They aren't normal baboons, that's for sure!" Akori reached the crown of the hill and stood with his sword out, ready to fight. "They must be servants of Oba!"

The baboons were surrounding the foot of the hill now. They squatted on the rocks and hopped up and down on the spot, as if they were mocking Akori. The three friends were completely surrounded.

Ebe hissed and shifted into her fighting form, the giant lioness-sized cat. Akori was glad, but also worried. Ebe would exhaust her reserves of power if she shifted form too many times. It would help now, but what about later on? He shook his head and prepared to fight. Later on could take care of itself. They just had to survive the battle facing them now...

With Akori on one side and Ebe the other, they braced themselves for the baboon attack. Manu hunted through the scroll, trying to find something that would help, but stuffed it away again.

Suddenly, as if they were obeying some order that only they could hear, the baboons all surged up the hill at once. Akori lashed out at the oncoming tide of grabbing, clawing bodies. Baboons were suddenly everywhere, screaming in his face, clutching at his legs, even grabbing at his sword and trying to tug it out of his hands.

He hacked at them, slicing through one and splitting another straight down the middle. It sickened him to have to kill like this – but he quickly changed his mind when he saw what happened to them once they were dead.

Every baboon he struck down instantly fell to the ground in a rattling heap of bones and dry dust. The remains looked like what would be left of a baboon after a thousand years in a desert tomb.

"These aren't baboons at all," he gasped. "They're some kind of baboon spirits!"

"They must be servants of one of the corrupted Gods!" Manu shouted back, hurling rocks from the valley at the beasts.

With Ebe clawing the baboons with her fangs and teeth and Akori defending with his sword, they were only just managing to hold off the creatures. But still, the baboons attacked wildly, as an unthinking mob, surging up the hill.

Akori was beginning to ache all over, not from wounds – he had nothing worse than scratches – but from the violent effort of hacking the baboon spirits down. Even Ebe looked like she was beginning to tire.

"We can't keep this up for ever!" Manu said, panting from the effort of throwing rock after rock. "They'll wear us out!"

"We have no other choice," Akori growled. *I just hope our strength holds out*, he thought. Already Akori felt exhausted and they'd barely made it into the Underworld.

Wearily he raised his sword to strike again – when suddenly a blood-curdling scream echoed across the valley. As one, the baboons turned and ran. Akori, Manu and Ebe all stared as the baboons scattered, hopping and scrambling across the ground, up the rocky sides and out over the uppermost edges. He expected them to turn and fling stones, but not one of them did. They simply vanished, giving the uncanny impression of obedience to an unseen commander.

"It's got to be a bluff," Manu said. "They're goading us. When we come down from this hill, they'll swarm all over us again."

"You may be right," Akori agreed. "We can't leave yet. Let's wait and see what they do."

But as the minutes passed and nothing happened, Akori had to admit that the baboons really had fled. The three companions were alone in a silent valley, with nothing but the bones of long-dead baboons to prove that the fight had even happened.

"Let's look at the scroll," Akori suggested. "What are we meant to do next?"

"I can't work it out," Manu confessed. "It says the only way to proceed deeper into the Underworld is to 'make a gateway from the bones of the Earth' and walk through it."

"Well, there are baboon bones here," Akori said, poking them with his sandalled foot. "Let's try making a doorway out of them."

But no matter what they tried, it didn't seem to work. They arranged the bones in a circle, in an arch, and in a square. But it clearly wasn't the right answer.

Akori stopped in his tracks. "What *exactly* does the scroll say?"

"'Make a gateway from the bones of the Earth'."

"It definitely says *of* the Earth, not *in* the Earth?"

"That's right!"

Akori looked at his own hand, at how the skin and muscle encased the bones of his wrist and fingers. If the flesh of the Earth is the soft parts like soil and mud, he thought, then the bones of the Earth must be the hard parts. Which means they must be...

"Stones!" Akori exclaimed. "The bones of the Earth are *stones*!"

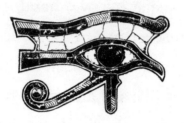

Chapter Six

Akori's excitement at figuring out the riddle didn't last long once the actual work began. It was a hard, tiring, sweaty job to drag rocks from the valley to the spot they'd chosen to build their gateway. He and Manu did all the heavy lifting, while Ebe – back in her small cat form again – kept a lookout from a high spot, in case the baboons returned.

At Manu's suggestion, they had begun building the gateway against a sheer wall of the valley. The rocks would be easier to stack, Manu had explained, if they had a wall to lean against. So far they had built two wobbly-looking rock columns to act as the sides. Akori wasn't sure what they would do when they needed to give the gateway a top. Rocks piled next to one another would just fall down.

Akori was moving three rocks for every one of Manu's, and his were bigger, too. He couldn't complain, however. Manu just wasn't as strong as he was. Priests didn't tend to be muscular, in Akori's experience. They were either as skinny as skeletons from spending too long puzzling over scrolls, or fat from eating all the leftover temple offerings. A Pharaoh had to be strong, though. How could Akori defend his people without strength?

Akori hoisted a big stone up onto his shoulder and carried it over to their gateway, which was steadily taking shape. It reminded him of his former life, working on Uncle Shenti's farm. Hauling rocks then, hauling rocks now – some things never changed.

"Are you sure we're doing this right?" he asked Manu, wiping sweat from his face. "I mean, nothing's happening. The rocks still look like rocks to me."

"We won't know until it's finished," huffed Manu, lifting a boulder the size of his head and adding it to one of the columns. "Till then, we just have to build it!"

Akori sighed, shook his head and went to fetch another rock. Then something caught his eye. There were hieroglyphs appearing on the columns, with the same weird red light that shone from the veins in the rocks. He rubbed his weary eyes, but he could still see them.

"Manu, did you do that?" he asked.

"No! Let me check the scroll..." Manu looked up, his eyes wide with excitement. "It's a match! Look, Akori. The hieroglyphs on the scroll match the ones on the doorway! That means we *are* doing this right!"

"Oh, thank the Gods!" Akori said in utter relief. "For a moment I thought all this work was for nothing!"

Now they knew they were on the right track, they worked even harder. The side columns were soon finished and they just had to add some sort of a top, to complete the doorway.

"What about this?" Manu suggested. He pointed out a long, flat slab of rock that was big enough to span the columns. The baboons had clearly been using it as a feasting table – it was spattered with blood and claw marks.

Akori tried to lift it, and just about managed to get it off the ground. "You're going to have to help!" he puffed.

Manu came and helped Akori shuffle the broad stone over to the gateway.

"Now we just have to heave it into place," Akori said. "On the count of three. Ready?"

"Ready. Just don't knock the side columns over or we'll have to start all over again!"

I really hope not, Akori thought. "One... two...three!"

Together they raised the stone up to knee height, then hip height, then – with a huge effort – to shoulder height. Manu's teeth were bared and his knees were trembling. "Can't...hold...it..."

Akori knew then he'd have to take the whole weight himself. He let loose a mighty roar and *shoved,* the veins standing out on his arms and neck. The lintel stone cleared

the tops of the columns and with one last heave, it slid into place.

Akori staggered back, a screaming pain in his shoulder. No time to worry about that now. The hieroglyphs were shining as brightly as a firelit jackal's eyes, and the space framed by the arch was wavering like the surface of a moonlit pool.

"We did it," Manu gasped. *"You* did it."

Ebe leaped down from rock to rock and stood alongside them. They hesitated for a moment on the threshold, unsure of what to expect.

"Well, good luck!" Akori said.

"You too," smiled Manu. "Shall we?"

"Together," Akori said. "Ready? Steady? Go!"

The three friends ran through the shimmering gate, right through the rock face and into pure, howling chaos. Akori could hear nothing but a continuous roar, like a waterfall or an avalanche. He, Ebe and Manu were flying – or falling – down a swirling tunnel of black storm clouds.

Akori somersaulted as he flew, helpless, like a tiny animal caught in a hurricane. The tunnel was exactly like the funnel of a whirlpool, or like the vortex that water forms when a basin is drained. *Manu got the spell wrong*, he thought in horror as they tumbled down the rotating vortex. *We're being swallowed up by some force of darkness even more powerful than Set and Oba!*

As the swirling slowed, the three of them tumbled back into the Underworld. Disorientated, his head swimming, Akori looked out at his surroundings. They were in front of a palace. Akori could only stand and stare. The palace was the mirror image of his own.

"Recognize that symbol?" Manu pointed to a banner that hung above the entrance to the palace. "You ought to. It used to hang outside your own palace."

Akori *did* recognize it – the red, jackal-like emblem of Set. Oba had used it as his personal mark, adding it to the shields of his finest warriors.

"Oba," Akori growled, gripping the hilt of his *khopesh*. "So this is where he's hiding!"

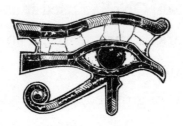

CHAPTER SEVEN

Akori was brimming with anticipation. "Manu, Ebe, look! We don't even have all the Pharaoh Stones, and yet here we are at the end of our quest!"

"I wouldn't be too sure about that," Manu warned.

"But don't you see?" Akori insisted. "We can strike *now*, when Oba is least expecting it!" Akori strode back and forth, swinging his *khopesh*. "He thinks I've got to collect all the Stones, but why not try it with two? We're here, aren't we? We don't have to do *everything* the long, difficult way. We can attack now, free Osiris, and destroy the threat to Egypt in one swift stroke!"

Manu shook his head gravely. "But this isn't the Hall of Judgement at all, Akori. Osiris isn't here."

"Maybe so," said Akori, "but Oba is, and I won't let him get away this time."

Without pausing for thought, Akori ventured closer to the palace. But as he drew nearer he saw it wasn't an exact replica of his own at all. It was more of a dark, twisted reflection. Where Akori's palace was decorated in blue and gold, Oba's was blood-red and sickly green. Akori's palace had ornamental trees outside, but Oba's had gigantic skeletal arms that thrust up out of the ground. The arms stretched out, grasping as the three friends passed by.

Where Akori's palace had pools, Oba's had circular wells of fire. The birds that sat on Akori's palace roof were scrawny vultures here. The statues that flanked the path up to the palace were hideous, with scowling demonic faces.

"There aren't any guards," Akori whispered to the others as they approached still closer. "Stay alert. It could be a trap!"

They reached the main gate to the courtyard, where instead of urns, the wall was decorated with carvings of snarling, monstrous faces. Their eyes rolled to watch Akori go by and their lips moved, but they had no way to speak. He wondered if they could pass on a warning to Oba, but soon realized they couldn't even make a sound. They must just be Oba's idea of attractive palace furnishings.

"There's nobody here at all," Manu

whispered. "No guards, no servants, no priests – nothing! Maybe even Oba isn't here!"

"He'd better be. I have a score to settle with that boy!" muttered Akori.

The gate was ajar. They slipped through into the courtyard, which in Akori's palace was green and filled with flower beds. Here, it was all dark sand and rocks, with spiked iron barriers around the outside.

Still no guards, Akori thought. *This must be a trap, surely*. Last time he'd sneaked through a palace like this, it had been to confront Oba in person. All kinds of memories came flooding back to him now.

The inner doors creaked open before them.

"Let's go to the throne room," Akori said. "You all know the way. If Oba's here, that's where he'll be."

As they entered the corridor, the doors slammed shut behind them.

"Akori, I think this is a trap," Manu stammered.

"I know," said Akori. "But we still have to see if Oba is here."

They soon reached the great double doors that led into the throne room. Akori nodded to Ebe, who shifted into her fighting form. Manu quickly studied the scroll, found nothing useful, and tucked it away again with a sigh.

Akori shoulder-charged the doors. They burst open, revealing a long audience chamber with a raised platform at one end. The throne that stood there was a gruesome, mangled-looking construction made from bones. The skull of a lioness topped one arm, the skull of a dog the other, and a dead falcon hung upside down above. Two skulls had been speared onto poles behind it, and Oba's banner hung between them.

Oba himself sat on the throne, smirking. Akori clenched his fists at the sight of his old enemy.

"Do you like my throne?" Oba asked. "It's a riddle. I wonder if a lumpen clod like you can work it out."

Akori glared at the skulls. "It's obvious, Oba. And twisted, just like you."

"Go on."

"You're mocking the Gods. The two skulls are meant to be Isis and Ra. The lioness and dog are Sekhmet and Anubis. And the falcon is Horus!"

Oba gave a slow, mocking clap. "Oh, bravo. I intend to replace the skulls with the real thing soon, but this will do for now."

Akori brandished his *khopesh*. "Remember this?"

"Of course. Tell me, have you learned to fight yet?"

"That scar on your chest is a mess," Akori scowled. "It looks like someone's sealed you up with burning tar. What happened to the nice clean wound I left you with?"

Oba's face crumpled into a sneer. "Enough. I'd love to stay and chat some more, but I'm afraid I have urgent work to do. What with preparing my army of the dead and planning the attack on Egypt, I'm a little busy."

"Not too busy to die," Akori shouted, advancing on him. Ebe and Manu followed behind, grim looks on their faces.

"Oh! Speaking of dying, I almost forgot. There's someone you just have to meet!" Oba snapped his fingers.

The doors burst open. Akori stood frozen to the spot as a monstrous horror came bounding into the room. It was a gigantic baboon, wearing armour and shaking a long club.

To his horror, Akori realized the club had been cobbled together from dead men's bones, human skulls leering at its peak.

"Now I really must go," Oba said, waggling his fingers. "Goodbye, all of you. I'd wish you luck, but there's no point, since you're all going to die."

Oba hastily slipped out of the rear door, closing it behind him, as the baboon craned its huge head down to peer at Akori and let out a bone-chilling howl...

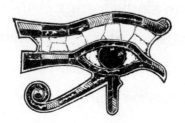

CHAPTER EIGHT

Akori knew in his heart that this was the
unseen thing from his dream.

"It's Babi!" Manu yelled. "The Baboon
God!"

Babi turned to Manu and snarled. Manu
gave a frightened yelp and backed away fast,
bumping into Ebe, who was arching her
back. Akori couldn't remember ever seeing
the young priest so scared of anything they'd
faced before.

"Keep talking," Akori urged him. "I need

to know everything you can tell me."

Manu gulped. "He's the lord of all baboons, in the world of the dead and the living. He's one of the most brutal, the most violent, the most bloodthirsty beasts in the whole Underworld."

Babi clutched his club in both hands, crashing it through a pillar before raising it above his head truimphantly. His huge shoulders hitched up and down and a vile hooting sound came from his throat. The God was laughing.

"He must have the next Pharaoh Stone!" Akori said. "That means I have to defeat him."

"You can't be serious!" Manu said, awestruck.

Akori swung his *khopesh* in front of him in a figure of eight. "It doesn't look like I have much choice, does it?"

Babi slammed his club down on the ground, rocking the hall with a thunderous boom. He gave a derisive snort, as if to say, "Very well, puny mortal, I accept your challenge."

This palace is built to the same plan as mine, Akori thought quickly. *That means I have an advantage, even if he is twice my size. I know this place inside out!*

"Come on, then," he said smoothly, biting down on the fear that surged up inside him like bile. "Are you going to stand there picking fleas off yourself all day? Or are you going to fight?"

Babi gave a furious howl in response. All around the throne room, doors burst open. The baboons they had fought in the valley came flooding in, clambering onto wooden benches, swinging from balconies and climbing arm over arm up the pillars.

"Now we know who was giving the orders!" Manu said. "These baboons must be Babi's personal guard!"

Babi began to chitter and screech, clearly barking out instructions to his bloodthirsty troops. They sprang to obey, some forming themselves into battle lines on the ground while others scrambled up to high perches.

"What's wrong?" Akori demanded. "Too scared to face me without an army? I challenge you, Babi! Face me one on one!"

Babi waggled his head at Akori and made a noise of sheer contempt. He seemed to be saying "I don't need to waste my time with anything as weak and pathetic as *you*." Then, with a series of long shrieks, he bounded out of the room.

The baboons crouched, ready to spring.

"Here they come!" Manu said fearfully.

Akori narrowed his eyes. "Run."

"What?"

"I said *run*!"

With Akori in the lead, the three companions charged back out of the throne room. The baboons shrieked and surged after them, the ones up on the pillars pelting them with lumps of stone and handfuls of filth.

"Now that I did *not* expect!" Manu said. "We're finally going to run away from a fight for once?"

"Oh, we're not running away," Akori said with a vicious grin. "We're fighting – but on our own terms!"

Manu looked completely blank. Akori explained: "It's Babi I want, not his foot soldiers. If he thinks I'm going to stand there fighting off wave after wave of his baboons while he gets to safety, he can forget it!"

Ebe hissed in delight and understanding lit up Manu's face. "So we're going to dodge around the troops and go straight for the commander?"

Akori grinned. "You've got it. Come on! We're heading for the tower. From there we'll be able to see the whole palace!"

They raced through the columned halls, with Ebe running in front. From behind came the furious sound of baboons tearing through the broken door to get to them.

On Akori's orders, they took a diversion through a set of rooms that were hospitality suites for visiting ambassadors in his palace, but here were prisons with chains dangling from the roof. From far off they heard the sound of thundering feet changing direction.

"They're following us," Manu warned.

"Let's fool them," said Akori. "Quickly, through here."

He opened a small door leading to a

passageway. Akori urged them along it. "Up through the next gallery, then right at the statue of Isis. The tower should be right in front of us."

But it wasn't a statue of Isis in Oba's palace, it was a statue of the grotesque Frog Goddess Heket; the tower was there though, and the baboons were nowhere in sight. Akori ran up the steps, sure that he'd be able to see a creature the size of Babi from the top of the tower.

However, as he cleared the topmost steps, he realized his search was already over. Babi was there waiting for him, standing on the ledge where the palace archers traditionally gathered to shoot at enemies.

"I think the baboons are coming up the stairs behind us!" Manu said. He hadn't seen what Akori had seen.

"I think we have bigger problems than that," Akori said darkly.

Babi chittered a hideous laugh and swung his rattling club in Akori's face.

Rattling? Akori took a quick second look at the club. Something loose was glinting inside the skull – he could see it through the eyes.

It was the next Pharaoh Stone!

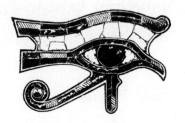

CHAPTER NINE

"Akori! The baboons! They're coming!"

"Ebe, help Manu hold them off," Akori ordered. "I need to get that Stone from Babi."

Ebe took up position on the stairs, her long tail lashing. Any baboons who tried to get past her would be torn to shreds – so long as her power held out, anyway.

"You've got something that doesn't belong to you," he told Babi. "If you want to give it up without a fight, now's your chance."

Babi gave his snickering laugh and hopped

down from the ledge. He raised his club high above his head.

"Fine," Akori muttered. "We'll do this the hard w—"

Babi flung his club. It cannoned into Akori's chest, flinging him off his feet and sending him skidding on his back across the stone floor. The pain was horrendous even through the armour. He felt as if a hippo had stamped on his upper body.

As Akori fought for breath and struggled to get back up, Babi came bounding over. He snatched up his club with one paw and swiped at Akori with the other.

The blow connected, catching Akori on his lower arm where the armoured tunic didn't cover and flipping him over and over like a rag doll. A sharper, scalding pain tore through him. Babi's claws had drawn blood.

The monstrous baboon strode back and

forth in front of him, making a big show
of licking the blood from his paw. The God
made hungry gobbling noises, as if he
wanted Akori to know how tasty his blood
was, and that he was looking forward to
much more.

He's trying to scare me, Akori thought.
*He doesn't know he's just making me
angry.* He rolled over backwards and
stood up, all in one graceful move. His
left arm burned with pain where Babi had
gored it, but he refused to let this show
on his face.

Babi rolled his eyes. By the look on his
face, he was bored of playing with him and
wanted to get this over with. He thrust his
club at Akori's neck, at the unprotected spot
just above the armour's collar.

But this time Akori was ready. He parried
the blow to one side and the club passed

harmlessly by. He stood, daring Babi to attack again.

Babi growled and jabbed with his club. Two more quick parries followed – then Akori was on the attack. Suddenly it was Babi who was retreating as Akori slashed at him from one side to the other. Akori whirled his *khopesh* around in a furious blow that would have taken Babi's legs off at the knee if the God hadn't hopped straight up in the air.

Babi was fighting mad now, screeching with rage. He held his club with both hands and instead of stabbing with it, he whacked it down in front of him. Akori brought his sword up to parry with milliseconds to spare, holding it above his head, keeping the club away from him.

Babi forced the club down on top of Akori's sword, his huge muscles bulging.

Akori fell to one knee. He strained to keep the blade between the club and his head. If his strength failed, the club would smash down on his skull with enough force to shatter it.

From the stairs he heard Ebe yowling, Manu shouting and the hoots and screeches of dozens of angry baboons. He prayed to the Gods to send them strength, because if those baboons got through, Akori would be overwhelmed.

The quivering club was now dangerously close to his forehead. Babi bared his teeth, forcing it down. Akori let out a yell that got louder and louder – and forced it back up. Babi's eyes became huge.

"I...will...not...yield!" Akori grated. He gave a sudden mad shove and flung Babi back, club and all. He stood, panting, unbeaten.

Babi let out a gasp and a snarl. Clearly, this opponent wasn't the easy victory he'd expected.

The two of them circled one another, jabbing, slashing, feinting. Akori faked a weak defence, prompting Babi to thrust his club too far forward, at which Akori slashed his arm before he could pull it away.

"Now we're even," Akori said. "Give up the Stone!"

"Grrrungh!" Babi spat, shaking his mane.

"Akoriiii!" came Manu's howl from the stairs. "There are too many!"

Time to finish this, Akori thought. He slammed his sword at Babi again and again. Every time, Babi managed to block the blow with his club. Finally, with a mighty yell, Akori delivered an overhead blow so strong that the club split in two.

Babi roared. Madness seemed to seize

him. Still clutching the top half of his club he leaped on Akori, wrestling him to the ground, sending his sword flying. They rolled back and forth around the tower top, locked in a deadly grapple.

Akori fought with all his strength, but it wasn't enough. They were soon pressed up against the very edge of the tower. The sheer drop below ended in rocks, next to a lake of fire.

Babi grabbed Akori's arm. He bared his teeth for a killing neck bite.

He's grabbing my arm, Akori realized. *Just like in my dream. I know what to do.*

It was then that Akori realized how he could defeat Babi once and for all. Mustering all his strength and concentration, Akori mimicked the exact move he used in his dream.

With a massive effort, he threw Babi across his body and over the other side.

Babi screamed as he fell. Then there was a gruesome *whump* combined with a sharp crack, and the screams stopped abruptly.

Akori looked down. Babi was sprawled on his back at the foot of the tower. But his arms and legs were twitching. He gave a feeble moan.

"The baboons!" Manu exclaimed. "They're running away!"

Babi was summoning his troops, Akori knew. "Get after them!" he yelled. "Down the stairs, fast."

They chased the retreating tide of baboons through the palace and out to the rear gate, to the shores of the lake of fire where Babi lay injured. The baboons surrounded him, uttering warning shrieks and swiping with their paws. They didn't want Akori getting any closer.

"You lost," he panted, leaning on his sword. "Give me the Stone."

Babi pulled the skull from the end of his broken club and fished the Stone out. It glinted turquoise in his palm. He held it up towards Akori, his face almost looking pitiful in defeat.

Akori sighed in relief. *Finally.* He stepped forwards to claim the Stone.

Then Babi let out a piercing shriek of spiteful laughter as he flung the Stone into the fiery lake.

"No!" Akori yelled.

The swarming baboons hoisted Babi up and carried him off, bearing their fallen king away from the place of his defeat. They scampered off across the firelit plains, retreating into the unseen distance. Babi's laughter echoed in Akori's ears all the way.

"You did it, Akori." Manu smiled. "You beat him."

"But it hasn't done us any good," Akori cried in frustration. "The Pharaoh Stone's at the bottom of a lake of fire! How am I ever going to get it back now?"

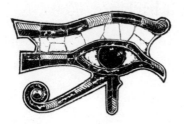

CHAPTER TEN

Manu quickly unrolled the scroll Horus had given them. "Don't despair. Perhaps there's something in here."

"May as well look," Akori said glumly. He sat down on a rock and looked out over the flaming lake. "I can't see what else there is to do."

Ebe jumped into his lap to comfort him and he gave her a stroke, glad that she'd remembered to change to normal cat size.

"Hey! This might be a clue! It's a

transformation spell!" Manu excitedly read it through to the end, then frowned in puzzlement. "'Know this, if you would be empowered. The devourer is not itself devoured.' What on earth is that supposed to mean?"

Akori thought about it. "I haven't the faintest idea," he admitted. "Some sort of riddle, by the sound of it."

"To avoid being devoured, you have to turn into the devourer," Manu guessed.

Akori scratched his head. "This place is full of hungry baboons. Do I have to turn into one of them so they won't eat me?"

"It might not mean that..."

"Well, I can't see any other devourers around here," Akori said with a sigh.

Manu looked around, as if he were looking for other devourers. Then he stopped. He frowned, deep in thought, then smiled.

"What?" said Akori.

"Go and stand over by the lake of fire, as close as you can," said Manu. "Trust me."

Akori did as he asked. The flames from the lake were so close, Akori's legs were growing painfully hot. "Well?"

"Now read the spell out loud." Manu held the scroll up so that Akori could see the hieroglyphs.

What on earth was Manu expecting to happen? Akori thought to himself. He began to read the words of the spell, glancing at Manu for help when he got stuck. As he read, the flames of the lake felt hotter and hotter. His legs were really stinging now. He thought about moving away, but Manu had told him to stand there, so he bravely stood his ground and kept reading.

As he neared the end of the spell, he looked down. To his horror he saw his legs were covered with flickering flames! "I'm on fire!" he shouted.

But Manu looked perfectly calm. "Keep reading the spell!" he insisted. "Just trust me, okay?"

Akori felt very strange, but he had to admit his legs didn't hurt. If anything, they felt *better.* Now the flames were spreading up to his stomach, his chest, his arms. They tingled and felt scorching hot, but there was no pain at all.

He finished the spell and stood there, a boy wreathed in flames. He held his fingers up in front of his face. Each one had a flame on the end of it, like a candle.

Manu's smile grew even wider. "You aren't *on* fire, Akori. You've *become* fire."

Akori began to smile too. "'The devourer is not devoured!' So if I *am* fire, I can't be destroyed by fire…"

He tentatively dipped his foot in the flames of the lake. It didn't hurt at all. In fact, it felt like poking a toe into a nice hot bath.

"I'll be right back!" he promised. He plunged into the lake and began to swim through the burning liquid. It was as clear as water, but the colour of lamp oil. The sensation was amazing, as if every part of his skin was alive with tickling flames.

Now he just had to find the Stone. He burst up from the surface like a human volcano and took a breath, then dived down as deep as he could.

There it was, glowing on the lake bottom! One final swim down, and he snatched it up. It throbbed in his hand, sending new energy coursing through him. He pressed it into the socket in his armour and began swimming back to the land. A strength he had never known before stirred in his limbs. All the fatigue from his fight with Babi was gone.

Thoughts of revenge raced through his mind. The Judgement Hall of Osiris and the remaining two Stones might still be far away, but Oba's palace was right here.

Maybe he should pay his old enemy a return visit after all...

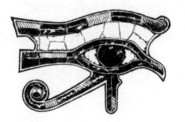

CHAPTER ELEVEN

Akori stepped out of the lake onto the blood-red rocks at the shore. The flames poured off his body in torrents. As he shed them, his body became solid flesh once again.

By the time he reached Manu and Ebe, he felt like his usual self, though much stronger than usual. The jewel now pulsing on his chest was the cause of that.

"You got it!" Manu said, leaping up. "Which Stone is it?"

"Strength," Akori said confidently. "That only leaves the Stones of Honour and Intelligence. But I don't think we'll need them for what I have in mind."

Manu looked troubled. "And what exactly *do* you have in mind?"

"We take Oba down. Now."

"Now?" Manu boggled.

"Why not? I have the Stones of Strength, Speed and Courage, and Oba's palace is right here! I already defeated his baboon bodyguard, Babi. He won't be expecting an attack now. Manu, we have to try!"

Ebe came bounding over and stood at Akori's feet, twining her tail around his ankle. "See?" he said. "Ebe agrees. Let's do it!"

"We can't," Manu said firmly.

"Don't say that!" Akori yelled. "Don't say it's not time to fight, we have to think, we have to plan! That's what you ALWAYS say!"

"Akori—"

"No! I'm tired of thinking, Manu. I'm tired of always doing things the long difficult way. This time, I'm going to go and finish Oba once and for all – and if you don't want to come, then you can just stay right here!"

Manu stood looking at him, trembling with anger. "I thought we left the old impulsive Akori behind when you put on the Pharaoh's crown."

"You thought wrong!"

"Decided to go back to being a hothead again, have you?"

"Give me one good reason why we can't go and fight Oba now!" Akori demanded.

Silently, Manu pointed at something moving in the distance.

Akori looked. It was Aken on his boat, slowly rowing his way along the river. He was nearly at the dark archway that led out of this section of the Underworld.

"That barge is our only way out of here," said Manu. "It must be nearly sunrise if Aken has come this far. Do you remember what that means?"

Akori let out a yell of frustration. "But I'm so close! We still have time – I could catch up later!"

"Miss that barge and we're stuck here for ever!" Manu hissed. "Did you manage to forget everything Horus told you?"

He hated it, but Akori knew Manu was right. If they stayed in the Underworld for longer than one night, the life would be sucked right out of them and they would join the army of dead souls. He stared up at Oba's palace with the last of the spell's fire still burning in his eyes. "This isn't over, Oba," he shouted.

"Ready?" Manu asked.

Akori sighed. "Yes. Come on."

Together they both sprinted away from the palace with Ebe racing ahead. Akori didn't look back once. There would be time for a rematch with Oba soon enough, he knew. Besides, Manu had spoken the truth. As Pharaoh, he had responsibilities. This wasn't about his personal grudges, it was about the safety of the whole kingdom.

The three of them leaped aboard Aken's boat. As Manu was climbing in, Akori laid a hand on his shoulder.

"Sorry," he said. "I lost my temper back there."

"I noticed," Manu said, pursing his lips.

Akori shook his head. "It's the Stone. It made me feel so strong! I felt I could take Oba on right there... I could tear the whole palace down around him."

"Here's something to think about, Akori,"

Manu said. "So far you've got the Stones for courage, speed and strength. But which ones *haven't* you got?"

Akori's cheeks prickled with embarrassment. "Honour. And..."

Manu raised an eyebrow. "Yes?"

"Intelligence," Akori admitted. "I'm lacking honour and intelligence."

Manu looked at him levelly. "You said it, My Pharaoh." Then they both started to laugh.

Manu was right, Akori knew. There was a balance to the Pharaoh Stones, and he couldn't win with brute strength, speed or courage alone. He would need all the Stones to free Osiris. There were other battles still to come.

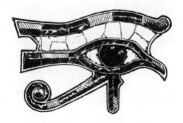

CHAPTER TWELVE

Akori, Manu and Ebe lay together in the darkness listening to the whoosh and gurgle of the water. Aken's barge was passing through the river and back to the upper world, to the Egypt they knew.

Akori peered over the edge of the boat. "Sunlight!" he exclaimed joyfully. "It's dawn. We made it back!"

"Every time we go down to the Underworld, I wonder if I'll ever see sunlight again," Manu said, stretching. Ebe arched her back and stretched too, the sun bright on her fur. All three of them felt relief that was sweeter than the finest grapes.

Akori lowered himself onto the deck and stood looking out over the Nile. Farmers' fields stretched out to either side in a brown and green patchwork. *Home again, safe and sound,* he thought.

"It's like the nightmare is over," Manu said. "Ra's in his heaven, and all is well on the earth below."

Suddenly, something broke the surface near the boat, snapped bony jaws and dived down again. Akori felt a chill of horror. "Did you see that?"

"What?" Manu was still smiling and admiring the view.

"There!" Akori pointed. The thing was rising again. This time, they all saw it. The skeletal remains of a mummified crocodile, swimming alongside them, water streaming out of its empty bone eye sockets every time its head broke the surface. Two more rose to join it, as if they were hatching out from the mud and filth below.

"The nightmare is *far* from over," Akori said, feeling shaken. "Oba's forces are still breaking through."

"They must be following Aken's barge," Manu said. "These things have swum all the way from the Underworld. The spells to keep them down there must have failed."

"I'm going to have to send messengers out. The fishermen need to be warned."

"You can kill an ordinary crocodile with a harpoon," Manu agreed. "But one of those things?"

"Let's get back to the palace!" Akori said. "The moment the barge gets close to the

riverbank, jump – and don't let those crocodile mummies touch you!"

They hastily made their way back. It gave Akori an uneasy feeling in the pit of his stomach to see his own palace looming up ahead. He couldn't stop thinking of Oba's sinister copy of it down in the Underworld, with its hideous statues, iron-spiked battlements and rooms full of horror.

Once they were inside, Manu turned to him. "We need to tell the High Priest about everything that's happened. Come on."

"I'll be there in a minute," Akori said.

"Okay," Manu said. "Come and join us when you're ready."

Akori slipped away to the throne room. There was nobody else there. The throne stood empty, waiting for him and him alone.

Less than three hours ago, he had stood in the Underworld version of this room, with Oba gloating at him and Babi ready to attack. He couldn't remember ever having come so close to defeat. If Manu hadn't solved the riddle of the scroll, if Ebe hadn't been so courageous and fierce, or if his own strength had failed, they would be in the Underworld still.

He looked down at the three Stones gleaming in his armour and gripped the hilt of his *khopesh*.

"I am more than halfway through my quest," he said to himself. Then he raised his voice aloud: "Hear me, all you Gods! I shall not rest until Osiris is released and Oba and Set are defeated. In the name of Egypt and my people, *I swear it!*"

EPILOGUE

Beside the lake of fire, a baboon stood on a rock, chittering and waving its arms. Oba waited with his arms folded. The baboon was only seconds away from being kicked into the lake and both of them knew it.

"I do not care how much pain he is in," Oba said. "Go and tell him this. If he does not present himself to me within the next sixty seconds, he will be in a lot more pain!"

The baboon cringed and scampered off. Fifty-five seconds later the creature reappeared at the head of a group of other baboons. They were carrying Babi, who looked up at Oba with a face filled with guilt and fear. The baboons dumped him on the lake shore and quickly ran back, huddling together. Babi lay on his back, still not able to walk.

"Well, if it isn't the most fearsome and bloodthirsty of all the Dark Gods," Oba jeered. "What happened to you?"

Babi made a whimpering noise in his throat. Thanks to Set's magic, Oba could understand exactly what he was saying.

"From the tower? I see. And where is the Stone I gave you?"

Babi hesitated, then made a tiny squeaking sound like the dying gasp of a bat.

"What do you mean, you 'lost it'?" Oba's voice rose to a screech. "It...it wasn't a sandal, or a toy, or a comb! It wasn't something you just misplace! It was one of the Pharaoh Stones! Do you even know what that means, you fur-covered oaf?"

Babi covered his face with his hands.

Oba delivered kick after vicious kick to his

sides, yelling all the while about how useless Babi was and how he would learn the price of failure.

A geyser of flame shot up from the lake, showering both Oba and Babi with burning droplets. Oba yelled in surprise and fell to his knees.

Set rose up from the lake, roaring in anger. "Another failure?" he bellowed. "Another Stone lost? Explain!"

"It was him!" Oba screeched, pointing at Babi. "The failure is his, not mine! I did everything right – I lured Akori into the trap – but Babi let us down!"

"Silence! Our enemy's luck is about to run out," Set growled. "I know exactly the God to enlist – a God so powerful and deadly he makes this fool look like the performing baboon he is! Once Akori comes face to face with him, our reign of darkness can begin."

DON'T MISS AKORI'S NEXT BATTLE!

CLASH OF THE DARK SERPENT

The Sun God has been captured by the gigantic serpent of the Underworld. Now Akori must defeat the beast, or else darkness will seize Egypt for eternity.

READ ON FOR A SNEAK PREVIEW!

Suddenly, the warmth on Akori's face disappeared. He opened his eyes and looked around. He could scarcely believe it. He closed his eyes and opened them again. But it was true. Everything had changed.

The world had been plunged into darkness. The sun had vanished and the sky was as black as coal. Not even a single star lit the unnatural night.

This can't be right, Akori thought. I must have fallen asleep. I have to be dreaming…

For almost a minute the world seemed to hold its breath. Then, from somewhere in the palace, came a scream…

ISBN 9781409562061

COLLECT EVERY QUEST

ATTACK *OF THE* SCORPION RIDERS

For his first quest, Akori must risk his life,
fighting giant scorpions and a hideous
Snake Goddess. Will he be victorious?

ISBN 9781409521051

CURSE *OF THE* DEMON DOG

The dead are stalking the living and it's up
to Akori to stop them – but a scary
dog-headed hunter is on his trail!

ISBN 9781409521068

BATTLE *OF THE* CROCODILE KING

Akori must brave the Nile to battle two
evil Gods – the terrifying Crocodile King,
and the bloodthirsty Frog Goddess.

ISBN 9781409521075

LAIR *OF THE* WINGED MONSTER

Vicious vultures and deadly beasts lie in wait
for Akori as he searches the desert for the
Hidden Fortress of Fire.

ISBN 9781409521082

SHADOW *OF THE* STORM LORD

Akori must fight Set, the dark Lord of
Storms himself, and beat the evil Pharaoh
Oba, in his deadliest battle yet.

ISBN 9781409521099

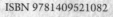

FREE GAME CARDS IN EVERY BOOK!

FIGHT OF THE FALCON GOD
Young Pharaoh Akori ventures into the Underworld to battle the fearsome Falcon God. But can he make it out alive?

ISBN 9781409562009

RISE OF THE HORNED WARRIOR
Akori must escape from the Underworld labyrinth of bones and overcome the lightning-fast Lord of Thunder.

ISBN 9781409562023

SCREAM OF THE BABOON KING
Akori journeys to Oba's Underworld palace, where he confronts his nightmares in the form of the evil Baboon God.

ISBN 9781409562047

CLASH OF THE DARK SERPENT
The Sun God has been captured by the gigantic serpent of the Underworld. Will Akori be able to defeat the awesome beast?

ISBN 9781409562061

DESCENT OF THE SOUL DESTROYER
Akori faces the ultimate challenge when he reaches the heart of the Underworld and meets the monstrous Soul Devourer.

ISBN 9781409562085

THERE'S A WHOLE WORLD OF GODS AND
MONSTERS WAITING TO BE EXPLORED AT...

www.questofthegods.co.uk

Check out all the game cards online and
work out which ones YOU'LL need to
beat your friends

Discover exclusive new games to play
with your collectable cards

Investigate an interactive map of ancient Egypt

Get tips on how to write top-secret messages
in hieroglyphics

Find out the goriest facts and grossest info
on ancient Egypt

Download cool guides to the gods,
amazing Egyptian make-and-do activities,
plus loads more!

LOG ON NOW!

WWW.QUESTOFTHEGODS.CO.UK